Poison The Well

J.K Divia

American Selkie LLC

Cover Design: Zooe Franci

Illustrations: Zooe Franci

Editors: Meg Adams, Chelsea McKenna

Proofreading: Chelsea McKenna, Kerry Kittle

Formatter: American Selkie LLC

Published by J.K Divia

Paperback ISBN: 979-8-9944702-0-6

eBook ISBN: 979-8-9944702-2-0

For permissions, inquires, or bulk purchase information, please contact @j.k.divia@gmail.com

To those who still seek comfort in the winding forest paths and in the forgotten tales rich with myth, folklore, fairy tales, and a little bit of horror.

Author Note

Poison The Well is inspired by Celtic folklore and mythology, in particular the Bean-Nighe or Washerwoman. It is not intended as an accurate retelling of any specific myth. This story draws on Irish folklore and history, including references to famine. While parts of this story are inspired by real locations, all parts of this story are fictional and should not be taken as fact. This book is a work of fiction. All names, characters, events, and incidents are either a product of the author's imagination or used in a fictitious manner. Any resemblance to actual persons, living or dead, or actual events is purely coincidental.

CONTENT WARNING

This is an adult, dark fantasy and horror novella with supernatural horror.
Readers should be aware that the story includes themes and references to
– but not limited to- death and dying,
violence and murder, body horror/de-
cay, grief and psychological torment, do-
mestic abuse, childbirth related death,
famine, and sexual coercion and manip-
ulation (non-graphic).

ALSO BY J.K DIVIA
A Sea of Blood and Tears
Berja
A Witch's Penance
What The Sea Knows

Contents

Name Pronuncations   IX

1. Chapter 1   3

2. Chapter 2   5

3. Chapter 3   21

4. Chapter 4   29

5. Chapter 5   41

6. Chapter 6   53

7. Chapter 7   63

8. Chapter 8   71

9. Chapter 9   77

10. Chapter 10   85

11. Chapter 11   97

12. Chapter 12   103

13. Chapter 13   109

Glossary   115

Name Pronuncations

NAME PRONUCIATIONS
Bean-nighe – ben-NEE-yeh
Emer– EE-mer
Seanmhair– SHENN-uh-vur
Sadhbh – Sigh-ve
Cillian– Kill-ee-an
Aos-sìth – ees-shee
Leannan- sìth – LYAN-awn shee
Baobhan-sìth – ba-von shee

1

As Cillian's bloodline weakened and his heirs dwindled, the beauty of the sacred well where he struck his bargain with Sadhbh began to fall into ruin. The stones around the well cracked, and the water from deep within soured, reeking of death and decay. The woods grew darker and more ominous, and the chittering of the other-folk grew louder. A bargain struck became a bargain broken, and a debt was due. The other-folk became restless, and their once quiet whispers grew into chants—and those chants into a command.

Steal the rocks and burn the stone.
Split the skulls and crush the bones.
Destroy the village and poison the well.
Muffle the shrieks and leave no one to tell.

THE WASHERWOMAN

2

The water is never still for long.

When the tiny bubbles appear, like a pot simmering before it boils, I know a death is coming.

I always know.

I also know what I must do.

When the simmer turns to a rolling boil, the water brings me the clothes of those marked for death.

I dip my hands into the water, as I have done so many times before. The beginning and the end of this chore have become the same. There is no measure for time here, no changing of the seasons, not even the rising or setting of the sun.

Some stories say a lifetime in their world would be but a fleeting moment in ours. Others say a single day in their world costs you a hundred years in ours, returning you to a world beyond recognition and leaving you alone to drown in grief. What is time to the other-folk but another one of their traps?

Though we know them as the other-folk, I've heard them called by other names—the dark ones, the fae, fairies, or the fair folk. I have never known there to be any fairness about them, though.

Only when I finally leave this place will I know which stories are true or not.

Stories are all I have now. I cling to them the way a drowning woman clings to a thin branch from a tree overhead as the water rages around her and she prays it doesn't break.

There is a legend that Seanmhair, my grandmother, would tell when I was a child. Many, many years ago, when long days stretched on and hard work was never in short supply. When our chores were done, we sat beside grandmother as she finished washing her load of clothes and linens. They belonged to the lords and ladies who lived in the old gray stone castle that lay at the edge of the loch. My grandmother's hands were wrinkled from the hours spent in the cold spring's wetness, washing outside the safety of the stone walls surrounding the village in the castle's shadow.

I still remember the way her voice sounded when lost in the tale she wove of the Bean-nighe, the tenderness and patience of it. Like a gentle melody playing against the sloshing of the water as she rinsed, and the pinging of the droplets against the wet earth as she twisted to wring the water out of the linens.

When I close my eyes, I can still see and hear my grandmother as if she was here with me now. Her memory brings a warmth that the icy cold waters of my pool can't drain from me, not yet.

"He was a great warrior," Grandmother would say, her hands busy with work and her gaze cast down toward the washing. "Handsome, true, and brave, one of old whose kind is unlikely to be found in our time anymore. One who fears not the dark woods, the monsters, nor the other-folk who lie within. One who fears not even death. Not even when he is warned and given a chance to change his fate with it."

We would gasp and huddle closer, waiting for her story to continue.

"The great warrior encountered a fairy girl, a Bean-nighe, on his way to battle. She was a small, beautiful, red-haired thing with skin as pale as milk and a glow like moonlight. She sat upon a mossy stone, weeping and singing a mournful song as she hunched over a lonely stream and washed a bundle of blood-stained clothes. The warrior recognized the clothes as his and his alone, and knew she cried for him. Brave and fierce, he continued to the battle, not deterred by the knowledge that he would die that day. For a great name earned in battle, he believed, was worth more than a long life."

I open my eyes, and I'm left with nothing but the ripples of the water I create with my fingers as I reach down to stroke the surface. The comfort tied to the memory of her voice fades into the darkness and silence that are ever-present in this world I'm trapped in.

I am left thinking how he was right, the warrior.

For in the end, we are nothing more than memories turned to stories, and only the ones whose stories are passed down are the ones who live forever.

Even as a child, I wondered if anyone would weep for me when I was dead and buried. If anyone would tell my story.

Before our love grew from that of childhood friendship into something closer and more intense, I was already thinking of Finn. Finn, whose presence always lingered like the stain and scent of summer berries on your fingers long after the fruit was gone.

Finn was like me, and maybe that is why we were drawn to each other so early. His mother died bringing him into this world, just as mine had. His father remained, though, neither stricken by grief nor the tricks of the others. His father was a hunter, descended from warriors, cunning and clever and strong as they come. Finn was very much like him in that way, but his looks all came from his mother: raven-haired and eyes as dark as wood blackened by fire. His build was slighter than that of his broad-shouldered father and brother.

He was brave in the way of heroes from old stories, defending me from the other children who made no secret of their dislike for me and my strangeness. While Finn was protected by his father's position as a hunter, I was not.

I could easily imagine him as the warrior from grandmother's story, and naturally, I saw myself as the beautiful fairy woman, the two of us forever bound by fate. I dreamed that instead of riding off to battle, he would stop and stay with me by the stream, averting his death and banishing the ghost of loneliness that always hovered around me.

While I was lost in the daydreams of Finn and me, the other children would always ask about the warrior, his name, and the manner in which he died.

But my interest was always in the beautiful fairy girl—the one who performed the same mundane task as my grandmother and me. I think back often to my childhood and to that story, to how the other children would grab sticks and pretend to battle. When they grew too rough and their game threatened to spill into the place where I was washing, Finn would step in to fend them off. My grandmother would laugh, kneeling over the water, her gnarled and wrinkled hands submerged, looking as though they had drowned long ago.

I tap one of my twisted and knotty fingers gently into the dark water, creating new ripple patterns as I once again get lost in another childhood memory. The darkness softens, dissolving into the memory of green grass beneath an overcast late afternoon of a day that I wish I could live again.

I grabbed one of the cream-colored linens from Grandmother's basket to wash it alongside her, hoping we could return home soon. I had finished my chores and my lunch long ago, and the pangs of hunger had begun to force my attention toward the linens again.

"Grandmother?" I wrung out a small tunic for one of the children in the castle. "Why was the girl washing his clothes? How did she get them?"

"She is a Bean-nighe." Grandmother paused her washing. She placed her tired and calloused hands on her lower back and arched it into a stretch, her old bones popping as she did. Resting on the back of her heels for a moment, she dried her hands on the back of her skirt before bringing them back to her damp lap.

"What is that?" I grabbed another piece of linen from her basket to wash.

She smiled gratefully and caressed my face softly before pulling away to stretch her back again. "Some say a fairy; others say the cursed spirit of a woman who has either died in childbirth or with unfinished laundry. So, you must always finish your work, Emer," she admonished.

"I always do, Grandmother. And yours!"

I held up the last piece of wet laundry to show her before wringing it out. She rewarded me with the smile she reserved only for me, displaying fully her discolored and chipped teeth. The front tooth on her left side was missing, broken years earlier when she tried to crack open a roasted nut for me.

"Aye, you do, child. Most days, if you aren't distracted."

She pushed herself up off the ground. Such a simple movement, but something that had started to take more effort from her over time. I didn't want to think about her getting old. She was the only family I had, with my father having disappeared into the woods and my mother long dead. I couldn't ignore the creaking and popping of her bones, though, akin to the sound of old trees during a strong wind when she moved too quickly, especially in the morning.

Grandmother gathered the wrung-out linens laid out on the rocks, throwing them over her shoulder as she did. She rocked side to side as she shuffled up to the line, pulling down dried clothes and placing the wet ones in their place. We would collect these the next day, after the sun had done its share of the work.

The stream where we washed the clothes was cold and deep, and I had heard that it was fed from the very well where Cillian struck his bargain with the Leannan Sìth, the fairy woman who took men as lovers and became their muse. It must be so; no other water around the castle or the village was as cold. It's a wonder the stream never freezes as cold as it was. My hands had begun to ache from the work and the chill of the water, so I stood and followed her toward the line of linens.

"She dies either in childbirth, or without finishing laundry, or both, and that turned her into a fairy?" I asked. My grandmother handed me a basket of linens left to wash, made her way back to sit atop a large stone, and motioned for me to join her. The stone's surface had been polished and smoothed by all the washerwomen who had rested upon it through the years.

"She must wash the grave clothes of those who are about to die until she would have naturally passed away had she not died giving birth, or until someone finds and washes her clothes for her if she died with laundry unfinished." Grandmother breathed heavily as she rested.

It was hard labor, the work of a washerwoman. There was no one to take care of Grandmother but me, and I did not have the means at that time to free her of her burdens. I was stuck; too young to be married and too young to work for coin in the castle as the older girls did. I promised one day that I would take care of her and let her rest. Of all the women I knew, she deserved rest more than any of them. She took care of not just me, but of everyone lucky enough to cross her path. That is why they called her Seanmhair, Old Mother. Still, we got by, and she did her best to ensure others did, too. She said it was our duty to care for others and offer kindness. At times, I wished I had her to myself, instead of having to share her with the village. I knew that even when I could grant her the rest she deserved, there was no stopping her from the work of a grandmother—loving those who needed love, caring for those who needed care, and giving guidance to those who needed guidance. I began to wash the last basket of dirty linens, giving her what rest I could.

"Is it always the clothes of the people who see her? Does she cause them to die?" I continued to work the linen in the water.

Grandmother placed one of her tired hands on my back and began to rub gently, knowing all too well the soreness and stiffness that came with such unforgiving work. "No child. Sometimes it's theirs, sometimes it's that of someone close to them, or a warrior or chieftain of their clan. She gives them a warning of what's to come, a chance to prepare."

"Is there any way to prevent them from dying? Can she warn them or prevent it?" I sat up straight, meeting her kind eyes, truly curious.

"Some say that if you sneak up on a Bean-nighe, you can force her to answer any questions you have or bid her for a favor to spare the life of the one about to die, or ask her about your future. She can even be commanded if someone takes hold of her breast, suckling as a babe and claiming to be her foster child."

"Eww." I scrunched my face in disgust.

"Aye." She chuckled. "But if they are successful in binding themselves to her in this way, the Bean-nighe will give them any knowledge they desire. And some say that they can even command her to stop her washing, sparing the life of whose linen she holds. Unless it's that of their enemy, then they can bid her to continue."

"That does not seem fair, to spend eternity washing clothes just because you died without finishing your laundry." Guilt bit at me as I realized that my grandmother would likely be washing until the day she died.

"Life often is not fair, child. Now help me finish, so I do not become a Bean-nighe and haunt the lonely forest streams waiting to wash your grave clothes!"

"Don't worry, I would finish your laundry for you if you died." And when I told her that, I had meant it. I wrung the linen in my hands one last time before untwisting it and laying it flat on the rocks.

"Sweet child, I believe that you would." She reached out a single finger to caress my cheek as she often did, looking at me in a way that told me I was the single most precious thing she had left in the world.

I think about Grandmother often. And though there is no way to measure time here, beyond the changing of the souls whose linens grace my pool, I still remember that day, that conversation, as if it just happened. Grandmother's laughter, the cold stream, and the way Finn's name was never far from my mind or heart.

Grandmother was all I had once, until Finn. My father followed my mother into death soon after. He vanished into the woods, undone by grief, loneliness, and a touch of madness. Though some whisper he was lured into the woods by one of the other-folk; a Baobhan-Sìth, perhaps appearing as a beautiful woman in a green dress, using her beauty to prey on such weaknesses when the opportunity arises.

Before I died, I thought the endless chore of laundry was the punishment for a Bean-nighe.

I was wrong.

Now my whole world is this pool. This rock I sit on—that scrap of sky I glimpse from the small circle up above me. The occasional chittering from the other-folk that echoes quietly against the walls surrounding me. I sit on my little perch atop the slim and moss-covered rock in the middle of the pool where I am trapped, watching as the deep lines creeping across my fingers and toes grow. They deepen as they spread and the outer layer of my skin begins to bloat.

I wish I had kept Grandmother's story and her warning closer to my heart.

It is a sad thing to wish for a short life, but I cannot help but hope that if I did die in childbirth, that I would have been destined to die a young woman regardless, and that my time here will soon come to an end. If only I could remember where my body lay. Maybe it is surrounded by the washing I did not finish. Not that it matters now. Leaving this place, ending this torment, is the only thing I care about now. But if I could remember how I died, then maybe I could end this torment sooner. If I had died with my laundry unfinished, then maybe the only way out of this is to wash as many grave clothes that bubble up as quickly as I can.

I wear a trail of reddened and raw skin as the tears flow freely down my face, and the dark water around me begins to stir. I wish I could remember the last face I saw before I died, and I hope that it was Finn's. That I was not alone when it happened.

Soon, a bright, red-stained shirt emerges from the depths of the pool and floats on the water's surface. I slide off my rocky perch and wade into the water. I grab the shirt with one hand, and my world turns upside down as I am transported to another world and time. Emerging from the other end of the watery portal, I find myself in the middle of a lonely stream in a world not unlike the one that was once mine, a world of the living. I trudge to the side of the stream, crouch down upon the bank, and begin my work, mourning those who are about to die. And I fear that one day, the water will bring me the clothes of someone I love.

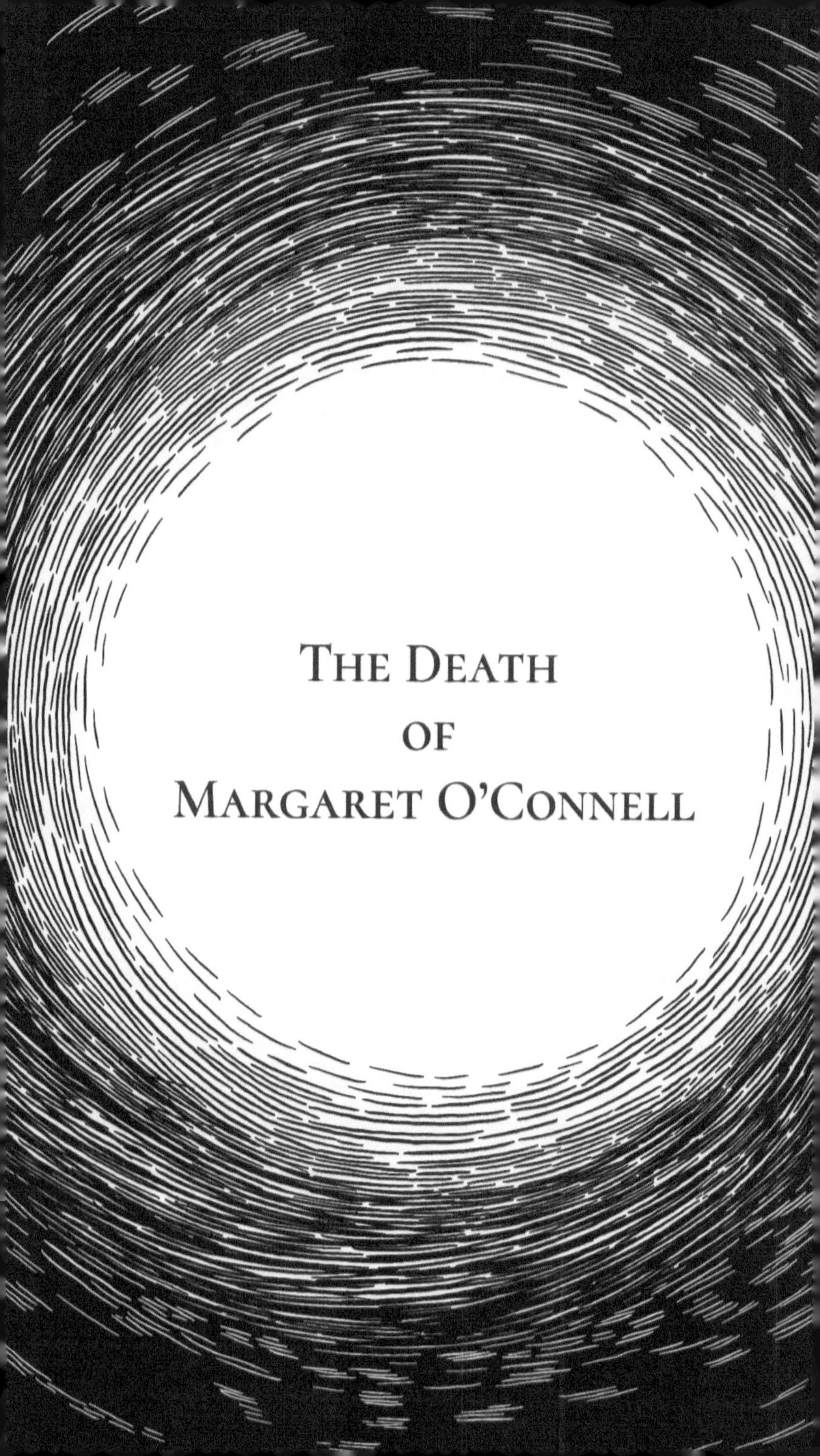

THE DEATH
OF
MARGARET O'CONNELL

3

For me, time does not march forward. It folds back on itself like wet linen, and I am helpless to navigate it, forever trapped amongst its wrinkles and folds, lacking both free will and any sense of control.

And this, this is the worst part.

This is the true punishment.

From the moment I touch the grave clothes of Margaret O'Connell, her entire life becomes my memory. Long dark hair rippling in the sunshine as she runs carefree in her youth down a brown dirt lane filled with small stones and pebbles, lined with wildflowers ranging in colors from butter yellow to deep purple, laughing as she breathes in grass and flower-scented air.

Another memory floods me, one of safe, strong arms cradling her when she was a child no more than five, followed by the comforting smell of her grandfather's pipe as he reads to her by the fireplace. Her head against his chest as the lull of his voice and beat of his heart send her off into a deep sleep.

The memories now spin to more recent ones of Margaret. I can feel the warmth of the sun on her skin and hear the soothing song she sings to her chickens as she collects their cream-colored eggs just days ago.

She is from another time, one far different than mine. Here in my pool, the years blur, and through her memory, I am forced to feel the world move on without me. Margaret's clothes are strange, and her hair is tightly bound now, no longer free-flowing as in her youth. She will die at the hands of her lover, a man she has known since childhood. She has borne him no children, and he has brought her no coin. His fear, temper, and insecurity will be the fuel to the fire he burns her with.

Only in my mind do I have a voice once I touch the grave clothes; in their world, I have only song. A sorrowful song which draws Margaret toward me and further from the familiar path. She coughs and gasps, her breath ragged from the exertion of her trek and the fluid in her lungs from an illness. It's this that will cause accusations that she belongs to the other-folk and be used to justify her death by the hands of the man who claims to love her. She continues toward me through thick brush and fog during twilight, near the ancient forts she mistook for a fairy ring, in hopes of catching a glimpse of her dead mother's spirit.

I don't blame her. Many times, I had hoped to catch a glimpse of my own dead mother in the pools in the forest, but Finn had stopped me every time. I just wanted to know what she looked like. If I had thought fairy rings would grant me a glimpse as well, I might have tried them myself, no matter the cost. My mother and any faint echo of her memory are of no use to me here, and neither are the memories of the ones whose clothing I must wash, yet their memories are my torment, their deaths my only path to freedom.

Margaret's husband was neither brave nor quick of mind, but he was possessive, like a dragon hoarding gold. He was easy prey for the dark whispers of old folklore and often looked upon her with increasing distrust. He had warned her of the dangers of fairy rings and of the fairy folk, who were said to steal women and children, and swap them out with sickly changelings. She would not listen, and the true threat she faced was not the woods, but him.

I wish I could tell her what awaits her back home, that she will die within the week at the hands of her husband. I wish I could warn her of what is to come, the accusations, the abuse, before her eventual death. I'd tell her to run. I want to, and I try to force my voice to warn Margaret, but only in my mind can I scream. In this world, my body is not mine to command. The laundry must be done, the song must be sung, and the tears must fall for those about to die.

The brightness of the bloodstains begin to fade as I wring and scrub her clothing fiercely against the wet black rocks before me. The waters the clothes bring me are rarely the same. Unknown to me but familiar to those whose imminent death I warn of.

"Are you okay, miss?" she asks timidly from behind me. Her fear not yet overtaking her kindness, a hallmark of her life, which makes her fate seem that much crueler.

I cannot answer her; the rules of this nightmare hold fast as I continue my work, my song carrying the weight of her fate.

"Miss?" she calls again, her voice breaking, and unease growing.

Slowly, I turn and show my face.

She proves that not everything about Grandmother's story was right. I am not some beautiful, delicate fairy woman who sings sweet, sad songs for the dead. Not at all like I had imagined I would look like when I dreamed of Finn as the warrior and myself as the beautiful fairy maid.

Time is an unfamiliar thing here, unable to be tracked except by the changes to my appearance in the pool's reflection. I was beautiful once, I think. I recall the times that Finn would bring me crowns made from flowers he had woven himself while out in the forest. How he'd place them at my feet and swore that their beauty still fell short of my own. We were no longer children then. Both of us had grown into our roles as young adults in the village and were free to indulge in courtship and love.

Thinking back to when I first awoke in the dark waters of my prison, my reflection was only marked by the ripples of the water. My hair was long and full, my skin firm and untouched by wrinkles. The memory is as slippery as the slime-covered rocks along the pool's perimeter. I try to remember the first garment I touched; my hands were not yet gnarled. The woman had called me child, and the fear didn't touch her eyes until it registered what I carried, what I sang, and the meaning of our paths crossing. That was the closest I had come to mirroring the image of the fairy woman from Grandmother's story.

There is no mistaking me for beautiful or human now.

Grasping at her heart, Margaret's face goes pale. She stumbles backward, retreating up the hill, and begins to run because I am a monstrous thing, squat with long breasts and bones protruding underneath thin and sagging skin. I resemble more of a nightmare creature than a woman now.

Her gasping and coughing fade as she disappears into the woods.

Turning back toward the water, the bloodstains are gone. The water begins to bubble once more, and I am pulled back through the water as the world turns.

I emerge on the other side, empty-handed, and wade back to my rock in the middle of the pool that is my prison. Placing my hands upon the slick, lichen-covered rock, I pull myself wearily out of the water, wrapping my arms around my legs as I sit and wait for my next load of souls.

I sit and forget their joys, their sorrows, their deaths, though the feeling of mourning never leaves me.

I sit, and I try to remember my own life.

I sit and dream of when children grew into adults and became lovers, when I was living, and my heart beat with a burning passion.

I sit, and I dream of Finn keeping his promise when we were children. His promise of setting me free should the other-folk ever take me. I know they have something to do with this cruel reality, as I am now one of them.

I sit and watch as the wrinkles deepen in my waterlogged skin, as my once-full head of hair begins to fade into something stringy and sparse, as my desperation and longing slowly shift toward anger.

CHILDHOOD PROMISES

4

I remember the warnings from when I was alive.

How the other-folk lay their traps in the beauty of the woods, enticing you with the charm of a sunlit clearing, beckoning you to rest beside the still waters of a peaceful spring. No one knows where their portals lead, for none return as they had left, if they return at all.

I grew up in the village that lay just outside the gray stone castle. Legend said the castle would stand for as long as the line of Cillian endured. It was Cillian's prize, and his heirs' inheritance, for a bargain well struck with the other-folk. The spring-fed moat was nestled at the back of large, stone walls outside of the castle's reach, which were lined with creeping ivy that gently climbed ever upward in some areas, and swallowed entire sections in others. Some said the castle was built upon a fairy ring, and that the well was fed from a spring that the other-folk had once prized but had lost.

Finn said that was a lie, one of those pretty stories the lords told themselves. He swore the real fairy circle where Cillian had struck his deal with the Leannan Sìth lay forgotten in the woods. The lords of the castle would sneak off to the real fairy circle when the moon was full and high, hoping to meet a beautiful fairy lover of their own to leave inspired into greatness, as Cillian had. It looked like nothing more than an old well that lay within a small stone circle, crumbled and broken for hundreds of years. Finn had seen it once, when the moon was high and he was too restless to sleep. He snuck out as he often did on nights like this and felt the pull of the woods. He said the well looked like all the traps set by the other-folk, appearing safe and unassuming. Even the stones of the ring were mostly buried, and if one didn't pay attention, they could walk into its bounds without realizing it.

Such an unassuming thing, a well, but Finn knew better, and he made every attempt to make sure I knew better, too. He trusted neither the lord of the castle nor the wood. Finn would protect me, always.

It was here at the moat that we spent most of our days before we were old enough to be put to work. Grandmother and the other women would watch us, the children of the other servants, as they washed the linens and clothing for the house each day in the stream. The breeze would carry on it the sounds of gossip, song, and laughter as the women worked, especially on days when the carts full of dried fish from the seaside village arrived. Grandmother said the fish carts used to come every week, but as the woods grew thicker, the village by the sea grew more suspicious of the woods.

I had asked Finn once if they were all evil, the other-folk who resided in the woods. He said he didn't believe so, that he had seen enough to believe that there was good there, too, but that the shadows cast against the light made it easy to overlook the helpers if you allowed fear to take over.

Fear is such a human thing, I think, as I tap my finger on the surface of the pool, amusing myself with the ripples I create. I didn't have enough fear back then, and I wonder if that is the reason why I am trapped here now.

I had little fear then because I was so certain that Finn would always protect me. Also, I cared little about the politics of the island, and instead focused on my little life by the castle—washing linens and spending time with Finn. Sometimes, I would help the servants make the soap we used by gathering the ashes to mix with the tallow. Other times, I would lay the linens out to dry, keeping the wind from blowing them away. My eyes went forever upward, searching the sky for any sign of a brown and white hawk—my hunter's hawk.

Finn was always with us then, running with the other children and me. His father trusted my grandmother and the other women to help keep an eye on him until he was old enough for his father to teach him the way of the woods. Some hunters had dogs, and some had birds like Finn, who'd been given a hawk by his father. Once we became old enough for chores, Finn began to spend more time with the men in the castle, and I was reminded that he was not a servant like us.

Occasionally, Finn's hawk would come, dropping off a flower from the forest, or swooping down to steal a drying linen.

"Emer, don't let that get away!" Grandmother shrieked, pointing at the bird struggling to fly away with the linen it had just stolen.

"Yes, Grandmother!" I yelled, chasing after the bird with breathless giggles. I always knew where it would lead me.

"Ah, Emer, hurry! It'll have to be washed again if it keeps dragging it along the ground! Tell Finn I'll have his hide if he doesn't stop stealing the linens!" Grandmother shouted, and a round of laughter from the other washerwomen followed.

"I won't, Grandmother," I called back.

I stole a quick look back to see Grandmother's head shaking. She fought a smile like she did every time she spotted Finn's hawk.

On that particular day, the linen danced in the wind as the bird carried it toward the forest line. The bird disappeared between the trees, and I followed. I reached the spot where the bird dropped the linen into the hands of a boy and then landed upon his shoulder. The hawk let out a small screech on Finn's shoulder and then nipped at his ear, which caused Finn to laugh and dig into his pocket for a tiny bit of dried fish.

"Finn, why do you always have your bird steal Grandmother's linen? She'll get so cross with you."

"I know," he replied sheepishly. "I wanted to see you. It's been so long since we've gotten to talk or play." It had been months since we last saw each other. He was taller, boyhood stretching into manhood.

"Does your father know you are taking a break from hunting to play?" I scolded, trying to hide my pleasure at seeing him.

"He's busy tracking a boar." Finn leaned against the wall of an old watch tower that had been built during Cillian's time hundreds of years ago and had since been abandoned, like most of the original outer buildings of the village that the forest had since reclaimed. Finn's hawk fluffed its wings, swaying on Finn's shoulders. "It's too dangerous for me, so Breccan and I are hunting rabbits."

Breccan was his older brother. They didn't share the same mother, and it was evident by their appearance. Where Finn was dark-haired and slight, Breccan was broad and golden-haired. Breccan's mother had come from the castle, as did most hunters' wives—a weak thing, as Grandmother would say. When an illness had swept through the castle, it had taken the lives of nobles and servants alike, Breccan's mother with them.

Maybe because of that, or because Finn was so unlike the others, there was nothing as beautiful in the world to me as Finn. I felt an odd, guilty thankfulness toward his father for remarrying outside the castle walls. That single choice opened up the possibility for Finn to marry someone like me instead of being bound at birth to one of the fragile ladies raised for nothing but lineage.

By the time of my birth, the heirs of Cillian had grown more obsessed with the purity of their bloodline. Only those descended from the founders who arrived with Cillian himself were permitted to marry one another, sealing their lines tighter with every generation. Grandmother said the more heirs of Cillian cut themselves off in the name of preserving Cillian's legacy, the more the wood and other-folk who dwelled within sensed their weakness and began to reclaim what Cillian had taken for himself so many years ago.

Finn's mother had come from the seaside village, though it's said his father had found her alone and lost in the woods. She looked as if she had fought for her life against the other folk and barely survived. His father, already a widower, took her in and married her against the lord's wishes. But the lord was weak in both mind and body and could not command or control one as such as Finn's father. Soon enough, the lord was distracted by his own failure to produce an heir.

Grandmother and the other women whispered endlessly about the scandals of the castle, of the ladies who could not conceive, the obsession with a child who refused to come, and the madness the lord was slowly sinking into because of it.

Not long after his father had found and married his mother, Finn made his entrance into our world. A healthy child made from the merging of sea and wood.

A snap of a twig, and Finn and his hawk pushed off from the old tower, all instinct and with quiet alarm. Finn lifted his finger to his lips, telling me not to make a sound and then gently guided me to stand behind him. The hawk took off from his shoulder and circled above twice before returning, signaling to Finn that all was well. Only then did Finn ease, allowing me to step out from the shelter of his shadow.

The forest was as beautiful as it was threatening, and because of that, we were rarely allowed near it because of the dangers that lurk inside. There was always an eerie sense of being watched from the tree line as we washed clothes. Usually, we would forget the feeling, having become used to it, but now and then a shadow would move between the trees that sent your stomach into a cold plunge, and the hair would rise on the back of your neck, reminding us that a danger was still nearby. Only the hunters were brave enough to venture in.

I did not fear it enough back then. With Finn's hawk guiding me toward him, I felt immune to any perils that the wood held. How could anything hurt me with Finn nearby?

I broke the silence between us after Finn relaxed. "Grandmother said it's dangerous here, but how can something this beautiful be dangerous?" I mused. "It smells of flowers and dirt, and it's much better than the castle."

"The most beautiful places, faces, and objects are the most dangerous." Finn let his fingers trace lightly over the brick of the old tower. "The fair folk lay the cleverest traps amongst the most splendid and appealing of things."

"Are you sure they're real? I've never seen one."

"They are real." He turned suddenly serious. "And they will take people away if they fancy them."

"Do you think they would fancy me?" I felt a sudden rush of excitement, followed by a flicker of fear at the thought.

"I would never let them take you away, and if they did, I would fight every last one of them to bring you back." A faint blush spread across his cheeks, and it pleased me.

"Do you promise, Finn?" My heart beat fast and a pleasant warmth spread within my body.

"I do." He handed me back the linen and a small purple thistle.

I took the linen and flower and looked down at my feet. "How do you know when there is a trap?"

"The traps look wondrous," Finn explained. "They appear real, but they aren't. You have to ground yourself in what you know is real, even if it is unpleasant. Like when I see and hear the leaves rustle, I have to stop, close my eyes, and see if I actually feel the wind. When the sun is shining, do I feel its warmth? Can I smell the scent of the flowers or taste the sweetness of the berries?"

"Do they ever try to trick you?" A kernel of fear grew in the pit of my stomach.

"They try. Sometimes I hear you calling my name, but I know it can't be you." He leaned forward and planted a kiss upon my cheek—our first kiss. Fear melted into excitement and surprise. The moment forever burned into my memory.

A whoop of a man's voice interrupted our meeting, and I hoped that it was merely a fairy trick so that I could spend more time with Finn.

"Is that really Breccan?" I asked, a little too breathlessly.

Finn laughed. "Yes, doesn't his voice pain your ears? That's how I can tell."

He walked me the short distance to the tree line, careful with every step he placed and keeping us on a clear path. Then he left, disappearing behind green foliage to rejoin Breccan.

In the days that followed, I would often search the sky, hoping his brown and white flecked hawk would appear to steal another linen and lead me to him once more. On days when young love urged recklessness, I would sneak down to the tree line and search for any sign of him. Catching a glimpse of him was worth the risk of punishment from getting caught either by Grandmother or the other-folk.

I would dream of another kiss, but I would have to wait years until we would be together as man and wife. Hunters aren't supposed to marry servants, but Finn, like his father, was never one to follow rules he didn't agree with. His father didn't care who Finn married, and though he was troublesome to her at times with the stealing of the linens and my attention, my grandmother held a fondness for him. He would continue to promise to save me, protect me from all the dangers of the world. I had never once doubted him, until now.

I look up from my pool, darkness surrounding me, and wonder how much longer must I wait for this task to end. Were all the promises Finn made me lies? Surely, he would have come for me by now. Maybe he's dead, or perhaps he just forgot. Or maybe his promises were never meant to last, nothing more than another story told to keep a girl quiet and waiting.

THE STARVING
OF
BRIDGET MURRAY

5

The pool ripples and the grave clothes start to bubble, drawn up from the depths of my watery prison. Once again, I crawl off my perch and slide into the water, reaching one hand beneath the surface to grasp the fabric that pulls me swiftly into another world. The location, the time, the people—they constantly change. But the water remains the same no matter where the grave clothes take me.

The heartbeat of Bridget Murray does not quicken, nor does her breath catch. She does not emit the same fear that all the others whose deaths I came to warn of did. All is calm within her as she drops the few meager roots she had managed to loosen from the earth where she stood and slowly walks toward me. She sits down beside me, and lays her head upon my shoulder. If I had breath to gasp, the air around us would have quickly been sucked in and held prisoner in my lungs. Her touch is at first like the sting of a bee, shocking and painful, but soon the shock fades, and the weight and warmth from her head feels like the echoes of a hug from a loved one. I wish for it to never end. To stay like this with her for eternity. I give no hint that her touch has affected me so, and she gives no indication that she is aware of how much it means to me, how much I have longed for the touch of another. Instead, she sits quietly until finally breaking her silence.

In a hoarse whisper, she asks, "What took you so long?"

I think back to Grandmother and her desire to always give what she could. Without intending to, I have given Bridget some small comfort in knowing that death has come for her finally, but she has given me more in return. She has given me touch, kindness, and comfort in this one small, fleeting moment of my existence as a Bean-nighe.

It doesn't matter the time or place that the clothes pull me too, the injustices and fear remain the same. This time, it is different; this time, there is no more fear, no more struggle, only an acceptance of fate.

Bridget holds no anger, no rage toward the well-fed men who sit in their grand houses, unaffected by the famine caused by their hand. She is beyond that. Her anger has long faded into weariness and longing. Longing to return to a time when hunger and pain were less prevalent and to a place where she could finally rest. She knows deep in her soul that try as they might, those men could neither crush the spirit nor kill the legacy of her people.

I sing, and I wash until her heartbeat fades. Her head slides off my shoulder, and her body slumps over into my pool.

How long has it been since I've been touched?

The water begins to stir, and I know I will be pulled back to my prison, but I do not wish this time with her to end. As the water takes me, I grab her hand, in selfishness and desperation to keep her with me, either her body or, better yet, her soul. But she is meant for a better afterlife than I am. She disappears from my grip and passes on elsewhere. The world turns upside down, and I am once again alone in my pool.

Back in the dark and freezing waters, I scream, I slap the water, and I curse the other-folk. I pull myself out of the pool and walk into the darkness until I hit the cold stones that encircle this pool. How many times have I searched this wall for an escape? Walking over and over again in a dark circle, pushing on stones, trying to climb, only to fail every time. Has it been years, centuries, or days? Time jerks me forward and backward through the garments in the pool and there is no way for me to know how long I've been imprisoned or how much longer I must remain so. I curse the men who seek to trick and steal what could never be rightfully theirs. I wail and I scream until my voice and body become nothing but rage, the only freedom this prison allows.

I bang my fists on the stones until they throb with pain, and then I rest my forehead against the wall in defeat. The water bubbles, and I know what comes next. I approach the pool, kicking the water as I enter it. The water splashes back at me, and I hear an echo of my grandmother's voice, admonishing me for kicking over a woman's laundry. This time, her voice does not fill me with warmth, but with shame.

Seanmhair's voice pulls me back to a memory of another day long ago.

Her name was Liera, only a few years older than me, and heavily pregnant with Breccan's child. They had been married the spring before. I never liked her; she had a mean streak, loved to tease and gossip, and stirred up trouble for her own entertainment. She would brag about her thick golden locks and how Breccan would say she had the hair of a princess. Since childhood, I had been a particular favorite of hers to torment. Finn had broken up our fights more than once, and as we grew older, her poor treatment of me had led to a souring between Finn and Breccan.

That day I had returned once again from fetching a linen Finn's hawk had taken, and Liera launched into me immediately.

"We ought to make Finn a whistle to call his dog. Sending the bird only makes more work for the rest of us." Liera smirked as I took my place next to Grandmother. I did my best to quell the anger rising inside of me.

Liera thought herself untouchable since marrying Breccan. As the first washerwoman to marry a hunter, she didn't much like the idea of Finn marrying me in a few short months, as if my marriage would somehow diminish the elevated new position she fancied herself in. She didn't realize the bitter truth—that we would always be washerwomen no matter who we married. There was no elevation in our community for those who lacked the blood of Cillian.

She threw a stick at me. "Go on and fetch it then like a good dog." Liera and a few of the younger washerwomen began to chuckle.

"That's enough, Liera," my grandmother warned.

"We're just having a bit of fun, you old hag," Liera sneered.

Everyone fell silent; a few shook their heads. Liera had gone too far, for no one ever spoke to Seanmhair, grandmother to all, in that way.

"*Take. It. Back*," I demanded, standing up and trembling with rage.

"So, the little dog barks as if it's a wolf." Liera placed her hand on her hips. She was bigger than me, taller and heavier boned. When we were younger, she had often pushed me down with ease or knocked my linens into the mud so that I would have to rewash them. I was scared of her then, like a sapling afraid of the howling wind, and I rarely fought back. But her disrespect of my grandmother filled me with a fury that I had never known could exist within me.

"Take it back," I said again.

Her smile only grew more wicked, and her eyes dared me to take action against her.

In anger, I marched over to her basket and kicked her laundry to the ground. The satisfaction of her eyes widening in shock only encouraged me to continue, and I stepped on her linens with my dirty feet, even picking some of them up and throwing them as hard as I could into the stream. I should have been ashamed of my tantrum, but it felt good, and I relished every bit of the destruction.

"You wretch!" She stood up and crossed the distance to where I stood half in and out of the stream. She struck me hard, then drew her hand back to hit me again, but I caught it before it reached my skin. With the strength of years of swallowed rage, I held her arm forcefully, refusing to let it move. She opened her mouth in disbelief, but before she could launch another attack, she doubled over and clutched her stomach in pain.

"Get her back to the village," my grandmother ordered. She moved much quicker than I had thought was possible for her and grabbed me by the ear. "You've no idea what danger you've put her in, child. Clean it up, all of it, for this chore is now yours, and what is left undone will be carried by you alone if it's not set right!" Then she followed Liera and the ladies fussing behind her back to the village.

I fumed. Why should I finish her laundry? Liera had been a bad seed from the start. But I tried to do as I was told, not for Liera, but to seek forgiveness from my grandmother. I waded deeper into the cold stream, the chill seeping into my bones, and gathered the linens I had thrown in the water. It was strange how they floated instead of sinking, drifting only slightly downstream, as if the cold had frozen the current itself. I collected all the linens from the water and muddy ground. I rewashed everything, wrung each piece out, dutifully hung them all up to dry, save one piece that caught on a strong gust of wind as I went to hang it. My instinct was to reach for it, to chase it, and I did. I chased it all the way to the crowded tree line, but once it disappeared into the forest, I stopped.

Fate is what I told myself—fate was the reason that linen was swept away and the laundry incomplete. Hers, not mine. It wasn't until now that I realized how wrong I had been.

Liera died in childbirth, and though the child survived, it was weak. The shadow of death lingered, casting fear over the child where there should have been joy. Word had spread as gossip does—everyone knew I was to blame for what had happened. Breccan would never look at or speak to me again. I no longer existed to him, and by extension, neither did Finn.

I was afraid Finn would hate me and break off the betrothal for what I had done to his brother's wife, for damaging the bond with his brother, but he never spoke of it, nor of what followed. He behaved as if nothing had happened, even after I confessed to the piece that had been carried off by the wind. I knew that there was nothing I could do to turn his heart, no matter how wretched I acted. I was far from the most wicked of things he had seen in the forest.

That was back when I was alive, though. Would he still love me now? Would I still be less wicked than all the things he had encountered before? In my heart, I know the answer is no. That may be why he has not come for me yet. Perhaps he lied, and I was, and am too wretched.

I fade out of the memory and am left alone with thoughts of that day with Liera. I wonder if I would have damned her to this same fate? Or in that small act against her, did I damn myself instead?

The grave clothes wait for me in the pool. What would happen if I left them so?

I have never tried, not once. Not yet.

I know I must finish the laundry, every piece of it, if I ever hope to leave this place.

I must face the truth that no one is coming to save me. I must save myself.

I reach for the garment and hesitate, my outstretched fingers lingering just inches from the grave clothes. But hesitation just prolongs my sentence, and I begin to think that it is not wickedness the well remembers, but what we have left undone. I grab the linen and let the world turn once more.

THE DEATHS
OF
THE BEAR MEN OF EINAR

6

The rules were never explained to me beyond what I learned from Grandmother's story.

Rather, they were slowly revealed by the bounds and limits of my abilities and confines.

I wash.

I sing.

I cry.

I remember their lives as I mourn them. When I finish, and they are forewarned, I am brought back to my dark little pool. This is the way it has been since I first woke up, floating face down in these murky waters.

That is the way it has always been.

Until now.

The water begins to churn and bubble angrily like a poisoned witch's brew inside a heavy black iron cauldron.

Not one, but many grave clothes rise through the churning waters, bearing the weight of more than a single death. They belong to not one, but many, reaped together as in battle or plague.

This is the closest I have ever felt to excitement since I have been here. I stand in the churning waters, surrounded by grave clothes and unsure which one to touch. Maybe this is it—my final load of souls.

I reach out and touch the linen closest to me and am brought immediately to a stream with freezing cold water, one that I know.

I can feel it deep in my brittle bones that I know this place, these banks, though they are overgrown and darker, more ominous than I remember.

The crumbled stone walls that lie behind the water I stand in are from a village that sits at the foot of Cillian's castle, a place that had lived beneath the sun when it still hung high in the sky above.

This was my home.

Like me, it has long been in ruin.

Finn had said I was beautiful, and he had made me feel as though that were the truth.

But as I bend down, my breasts hang low from my body, getting in the way of my work, I wish I could remember if that were true. I pick up one breast at a time, heaving them over my shoulder, out of the way as the memories . . . too many memories . . . come flooding into my mind.

This is different.

This is new.

I feel as though I've had too much to drink, tipsy and giddy and filled with a reckless eagerness. Maybe my time has come. Perhaps this is how my torment ends, and I finally become free to pass on to a different place and rejoin my ancestors.

The memories are chaotic: flashes of lives and childhoods layered atop one another, shared experiences, feelings, thoughts carried just out of reach. They are not men. They are bears, bears that change into men, men who fight as bears. Their skins are slick with the blood of those they have slain.

The woods no longer belong to men; they belong to the other-folk. Cillian's line ended long ago. The men whose grave clothes I wash are learning what happens when men enter the places where the cruelest of the other-folk lurk. The other-folk they encounter look like little men, and they make quick work of these intruders, these bear-men of Einar. The little men fill their caps with the blood that flows freely into the ground, staining them red.

The clothes keep surfacing in the water as I scrub and sing, excitement continuing to build from the newness of it all and overwhelming my senses—from having so many linens and memories at once. From the prospect of finally fulfilling what has felt like an eternal task.

That is when it happens.

Someone grabs my breast, and no sooner does he catch it, he starts to suckle like a babe.

I am bound to old rules and forced to answer old gestures, whether I willed it or not. I had my part to play.

"Come now, child, who suckles on me as I do my work?" My voice is hoarse.

I . . . I have a *voice*.

How long did I rage against the prison of my body, wanting to scream, to talk, to warn those who were about to die, only to fall silent beyond that of the mourning song?

Now, I *speak*.

Now, I have power. I can feel it coursing through my veins.

This is the closest to freedom I have had since becoming a Bean-nighe, and lately, it feels as though I've already lived multiple lifetimes as a Bean-nighe.

"It is I, your child." The man continues sucking.

I chuckle involuntarily while struggling to grasp the new power this unlocks within me. The power to speak and the power to prophesize, and the power to stop death itself if so commanded.

"Tell me now, child, what is it you want that you interrupt my work?" I ask.

He unlatches his mouth, but keeps a firm grasp on my breast with his hands so as not to let me go. He smells of destiny, determination, and just a hint of fear. I know who he is, but unlike those whose grave clothes I wash, I cannot feel his memories. I cannot see his life through his eyes or hear his thoughts as my own.

"What do I need to create the new world, a new land for my people and me?" he demands.

Visions begin to play inside me—different paths and futures of the man who commands me. A witch called Volva gave him the secret of how to find me, and how to secure my favor. I want to ask him about Volva. I want to warn him of what happened to Cillian and men like him, but though I can speak, I lack control of what comes out.

"Your light, your luck, has already run out, but then that was never your luck or light, was it?" I say, unable to refuse the words that come forth like water from a broken dam.

I continue to slosh in the water, washing and wringing the clothes and taking them out one at a time to beat against the bank beside me, unbothered and unencumbered by his grip on my long, snake-like breast that keeps us tethered to each other. The blood of his men flows so freely that the water I wring out runs red as I untwist their grave clothes and lay them to dry before moving on to the next piece.

The rippling water reflects the image of my gaping mouth, exposed teeth, and jaw blackened with death and rot. I am a frightful sight. Any beauty I may once have had has long since decayed beyond recognition. This feels like a new phase but the same torment. Surely my duty is coming to an end with the amount of grave clothes bubbling to the surface. I can hardly keep up.

"No," the man responds. "It was—"

Suddenly, the screams of his men break the quietness of the moment between us.

The man loosens his grip just slightly, enough to where I could break away if I wanted to. Do I want to? I think not because I must be close to the end. I need to keep washing.

"Tell me what I need," he demands.

"Tsk, tsk, child, isn't it obvious? You know in your heart what you need. You know in your heart what you lack. What you've always lacked." I continue my chore.

"Einar!" a man calls out.

The screams and sounds of violence continue behind us as lives end with the linens in my hand. I laugh, and giddiness begins to build again at what will surely be my last time washing. It has to be—why else would there be so many? Why else would I have these new abilities? I must be near the end.

"Tell me!" He pulls on my breast hard and squeezes it tightly as if he wants to cause me pain. I laugh, knowing he is nothing more than a young child throwing a tantrum.

"You need what you took for your own, used as your own, but was not truly yours." The words tumble out. My meaning is known only to him. "The only luck you can count on . . ."

"Is the luck you make yourself, you earn yourself," he finishes. I untwist and lay out the bloodied piece of clothing, another belonging to one of his men. He is nothing more than another Cillian. A man who seeks to take power from others and claim it as his own, so certain of his destined success that he scarcely notices what he has already lost in our exchange. There is always a price to be paid, an exchange for knowledge. He does not feel it yet, what has been drained from him, but he will. In time it comes for them all who make such exchanges.

"Einar, we have to go. Brothers are dying and . . ." another man says behind me, a man whose clothing has not yet come across my fingertips. "Einar, make her stop," he pleads.

"Isn't there something more you'd like to know?" I tease, knowing Einar is not yet done, that more questions linger in his heart. I can feel his hunger and ambition through the grasp he still keeps on me, and I do not want to stop. I can't stop. I need to finish washing their clothes in order to be free.

"Einar!" yet another man yells.

"Einar, make her stop or I will!" the man behind me declares. I hear the sound of a sword being drawn, as if that would have any effect on one such as myself. The only one who can command me to stop is Einar, and he is too close, his desire too strong to make such a sacrifice, to give up any knowledge of what he seeks to save his men.

"Stop now. No more washing," Einar demands.

His words are a dagger to my bloated, drowned heart.

I let out a heavy sigh. I am bound to the rules of the Bean-nighe and am forced to comply. Once ordered, I cannot wash again until the water reclaims me and the cycle starts again. I drop the linens in my hand, stand up, and walk into the middle of the stream.

So close . . . I was so close to ending my torment.

For a brief moment, I thought I finally had power, that I was on the cusp of being free.

The truth remains that I am but a slave of both my task and those who know the way to trap and command one such as me. Giving me a voice only for me to have no power of it and the words I speak.

Rage.

It courses through my veins, and if I could burn the world down, I would.

This Einar is no different from Cillian. They are men who build their legacies on bargains and powers not their own. They heed no warnings and bring others with them on the road to ruin.

Rage.

So much rage and no way to let it out.

Just the grave clothes, just the washing, and just the singing of the song of death.

The laundry controls me.

I surface back in my pool. I wade toward my small rock and pull myself atop it, letting one arm fall back to the water. With my fingers I trace slow circles across the surface.

As I watch the small whirlpool from beneath my hand, I realize I am in control of one thing: my joy.

Mourn the dead no more will I.

Now, I will celebrate them. Let the line of grave clothes never end their journey through my pool. If this is my purpose, then I embrace it and I will do my duty joyfully for this is all I have left and it is all that I am.

THE DEATH
OF
THE LORD OF MAC TÍRE

7

My pool.

My dark, murky, beautiful pool.

The water glides delightfully over my skin as I swim just under its surface, as I've come to do since the meeting with the bear-men.

I stir under the water like some frightful thing, and I think sadly how there is no one to see the lovely ripples I make. When I was alive, I would have dreamt of painting the world without misery or pain; now I've come to relish it, for it's the only thing for whom I now serve, and the only thing for which I am allowed to feel.

Lazily, I slide out of the water and stretch out on top of the slick rocks. I let one hand remain in the water, fingers gliding back and forth under the surface of the pool.

I hum a song of my own as I wait for the pool to bubble to life and bring me a treat of blood-soaked linen and a journey into death.

I do not wait long before the pool comes to life and a single tunic of fine linen and ornate embroidery rises to the top. Quickly, I scramble from my rock, squatting and cocking my head like a confused dog, staring at the finest grave clothes I have ever seen. This is new and different, and I tentatively stretch my arm out toward it, brushing it with one crooked fingertip.

That's all it takes and I am pulled from my perch and under the water, violently this time. The water rages around me until I am finally brought to the surface of a loch.

The times and places to which the water brings me have always flowed in steady motion, drifting through eras and lands with ease. This is the first time I have ever felt disoriented, dizzy even. A strange sickness coils in my gut. I stumble as I slosh from the water, clutching the tunic of a lord in my hands. An aging man whose rule will end by the treachery of others.

Once again, I am caught. I feel the grip of a hand on my shoulder, and his touch sends a shudder through my body. The visions I see of this man's future are that of my future as well.

This man did not seek me out as did Einar and his bear-men. No, this man was brought by fate—a fate which I am cursed to share.

This man is Cillian.

If I could have shrieked in fear, I would have. I now stand in a pool centuries before my birth, before my village, before my name was ever spoken. The pool has cast me here, to the first spark of a fire that will eventually consume me and all that I know and love. How can this be?

Cillian knew the whispers of the Bean-nighe. He had grown up hearing the tales of the other-folk from the crones in his clan. If you cross one and sneak up upon it, you can command it, bid it to speak your fortune, or give you a favor. Cillian took one sight of me and saw an opportunity.

"Those are the clothes of my lord, hag."

I jump slightly at the sound of his voice, which is neither filled with concern nor terror, but with possibility, and for the first time since I became a Bean-nighe, I feel fear flooding every inch of my body. Or maybe that fear belongs to the last remnants of Emer, still buried somewhere deep inside me.

"So they are. Would you have me stop and spare him?" I once again speak words over which I have no control, no true ownership of.

"What fate awaits me?" He is confident, capable, and handsome, and worse yet, he is aware of all these things.

The visions of his future bend and blur, before splitting into two destinies.

"Bid me spare the life of your lord," I say, "and when you speak of it, he will believe you. He can feel the chill of my touch along his spine, hear the fear carried in the whispers that tremble against his ear from my cold lips. Tell him of our meeting, and he will reward you with all you ask for. You know what you seek: a place of your own. There is an island, a castle waiting to be built, and a kingdom for you to claim."

"Yes," the man says eagerly, far too eagerly. For that is what greed does—it demands action without empathy and laps up opportunities without regard to ownership.

"But to make the claim, you must make a deal. A bargain bound for 300 years."

"Will I live for 300 years?" Cillian asks, excitement bright in his voice.

I laugh, such a human thing to crave an extended life when all I desire is a short one. "You will not live to see your kingdom fall. But if your line should ever break, the well from which your kingdom feeds will be poisoned."

"I care not what happens in a time where I do not exist," he replies. "It is enough for my name to be etched upon every stone in the kingdom I build."

"Be careful of beautiful words. Be careful not to ignore their meaning," I advise, but I know it falls on deaf ears because I am here, and I am the Bean-nighe of both past and future.

"That's enough, hag, the tunic in your hands belongs to me. Give it to me now, and be gone with you." He dismisses me as if I were nothing more than an errant child.

"The grave clothes belong only to the dead, not the living." I let out a sigh. I drop the tunic into the water and watch as it begins to dissolve. Cillian releases me, walking off confidently to tell his lord how he saved him, while I am pulled back into the darkness of my pool.

I return to the world I know and think what cruel fate is this, that I should be a part of Cillian's legacy before I even came to be.

I hiss like a snake before it strikes and angrily splash the water.

I am to be my own people's lore. I am to be the spark that ignites Cillian's fire, which will lead him to seek and find the island. Am I the fairy with whom he struck the bargain? Finn was right: the stories told are far prettier than the truths they soften. Yet the place where I met Cillian was not my home. It was not the well.

The well.

I have seen it myself, have I not? Once, long ago. The memory is blurred, a faint whistle of a tune almost recognized. I look up at the sliver of sky above me and force myself to remember.

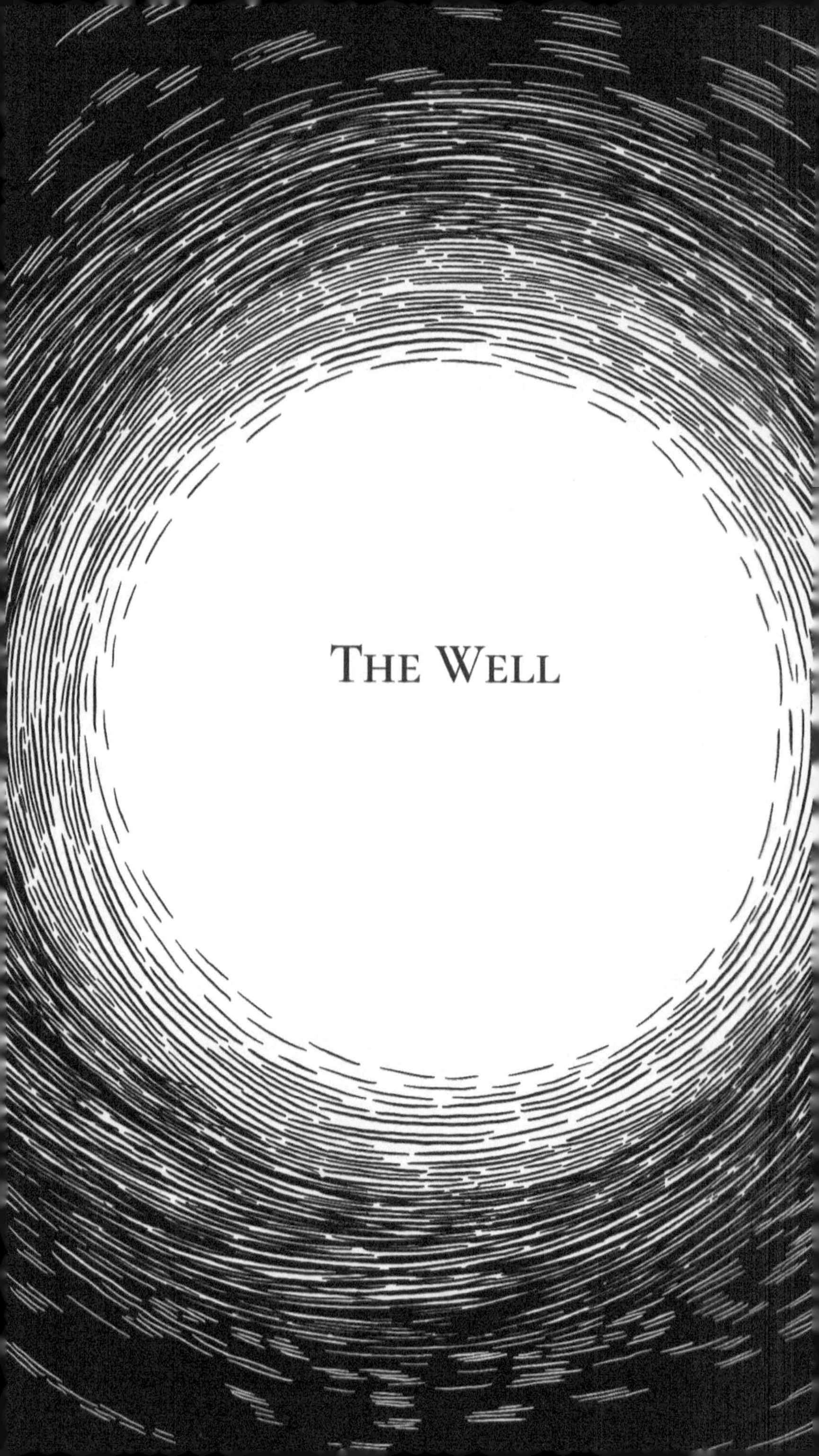

THE WELL

8

Remember.

I claw at the skin of my arms and shoulders, willing myself to remember.

I know I have seen the well. It lingers there, the memory, just beyond my grasp. It feels as though it belongs to another lifetime, before this pool, before death hollowed me into something . . . other.

Remember.

Closing my eyes, I push my bony, waterlogged hand to my forehead and demand the memory to conjure. It's fuzzy at first, like trying to see through dirt and tears. Scenes from long ago flash in my mind as quick as lightning across the sky in an angry storm. Flashes of faces I barely recognize appear as my vision begins to clear and the pictures become sharper. More faces follow, and then two I know well: my grandmother's and Finn's.

I focus on Finn's face, strong and handsome, but older than he has been in any memory I've recalled before. Finn's face also summons the feeling of my heart beating for someone I love. I hold onto that, and I swear the rotten organ inside me moves from a sluggish thud to something that resembles life as I force myself to do more than just remember, but to relive, to get lost in a dream with him and the shining sun, of flower crowns and stolen kisses.

But something is wrong. This dream, this dream is wrong. It's all wrong.

Finn's face is . . . angry?

He's yelling at me. He's squeezing my wrist and I feel the bloom of a bruise.

The world around us is shades of brown, green, and gray. My heart is beating too fast, painfully so. I clench my fists, my nails digging deep into the skin of my palms. If blood were to flow from them, I wouldn't care.

The old well in the forest, the mossy stones that circle it, the screech of Finn's hawk and its wings beating up above, and the crash of a broken jug. This memory is too much, and I want it to end. I move my hands from my forehead to my ears to try and drown out the noise, our voices.

"Don't EVER do that again!" Finn screams. His tight grip on my arm loosens, causing me to fall onto the hard ground.

"You're not my lord nor my master!" I hiss back, tears streaming down my face and making me even more livid. Because I hated that I cried when I was angry. I push myself up off the ground, stepping forward and striking him on the face.

I move to hit him once more, but he catches my hand.

"Don't ever do that again." He releases me and stalks away.

I am left with a broken jug and a broken heart. I watch as he walks away, and I look down at the hand that I used to strike him in horror. The memory begins to fade, darkness closes in, circling my hand until it swallows that up, too.

The memory is gone. Why did he grab me in such anger, and why did I strike him? I look down at my hand, no longer the hand of Emer but that of a Bean-nighe, and I find myself shaking. More tears stream down my face, and I rage.

He left me. He walked away and left me alone in the woods by the well.

I now know two truths at once—I can feel them both deep within my bones. Finn is not coming to save me, and I am not trapped in a spiral with an eventual end. Time did not pull me backward to Cillian; it folded me inward until I exist wherever I am required.

Bean-nighe is my fate and rescue will not come the way I had once believed. Maybe there was only ever one washer-woman, and she is me. With each new linen I pull, the further I drift from Emer, and the further into the washerwoman I decay until one day I am certain that all echoes of Emer will fade completely.

THE DEATH
OF
SEANMHAIR

9

There are many a fate far crueler than death, and this is one of them.

Yet I have embraced my fate.

I have even learned to love it. To find joy in the deaths, in the memories of those I was tormented to mourn. I have found a sort of peace.

But then . . . Then the game changes once more.

Over a hundred more grave clothes have graced the waters of my pool since I met Cillian, and I believed I had left all thoughts of my life as Emer safely behind me. I no longer linger on faded memories.

But the grave clothes that now bubble up are not of some stranger.

They are *hers*.

As soon as my fingers brush the garments, I know her again.

My faded memories come back in a searing pain.

But not my memories—hers. Memories of which I had a part in.

I see myself, pulled from my mother's womb by her steady and blood-covered hands. A wet and squealing thing was I—her love for me and sorrow of being unable to stop the bleeding of my poor mother.

It's not fair—any of it.

I want to scream at her, tell her to run.

I want to hide her grave clothes, as if that would prevent what is coming.

I can't.

I can only sing.

I can only cry.

I can only wash.

I see myself through Grandmother's eyes, from babe to woman. The times I caused her grief and the times I brought her joy—everything.

I hear her coming down the path. She will soon see me and know her fate.

Will she know who I am?

How could she, with how I've changed? When I catch my reflection, though distorted by the water's ripples, I can still see the monster that I've become, and I am ashamed.

I can hear the beats of her heart as she comes out from the forest canopy.

The mist covers the banks of the stream. It's late, mere hours from dawn and much too late for her to be out here by herself. She knows the dangers of leaving the village after nightfall and before the sun rises once more.

She has always done what needs to be done. Fear will not stop her.

She comes carrying a bucket of water. Water she drew from the old well in the forest, Cillian's well. The water from that well is the coldest, and some say it has healing properties. Few know where to find it. A secret well-kept, one that she is of a few to know.

Another woman is in danger of dying from her laboring, and not just a woman, but the wife of the lord of the castle, Cillian's last heir. Grandmother knows that the passing of this woman and child will only bring about more death. She feels a change in the air, and an unease in the water. She remembers the warnings in the stories passed down and knows that there is precious little time. She thinks of me, and what fate might bring if she cannot save this woman or the child.

She thinks she will fail me and her daughter, my mother.

Grandmother managed to reach the well, a feat for someone of her age. But the trek and the cold water strained a heart already worn thin by years of hard labor and heartache that comes from living to an age such as hers.

She was able to lower the old, wooden bucket and bring up enough water to fill the ceramic jug she carried.

A shiver ran down her spine; the woods were eerily quiet.

That is when she heard it.

The break from the silence into the quiet hum of a song from long ago.

Her body froze, and the ceramic jug fell to the ground with a loud crack, spilling some of the contents she had so bravely ventured into the woods for.

She knows the voice that sings such a mournful song. The rustling of the leaves in the woods does nothing to soften the sorrow carried upon the notes.

A gasp escapes her throat, tinged with fear and heartbreak, as she ventures toward the hum, unable to stop herself. She has to know. She has to see for her own eyes who sings and whose death awaits.

Farther and farther she goes from the well and the path that would lead her back to the village, her heart thudding painfully in her chest, and her breath coming sharp and ragged.

She knows she should run, but she has to see me for herself.

She has to know for sure.

Soon, the humming is joined by the sound of a babbling brook and the sloshing of water.

"Emer?" she croaks, almost choking on my old name.

I turn and see myself as she sees me.

The horror at what I am, the monstrosity of me.

"No," she says, stumbling back, hand pressing to her chest.

I want to tell her to grab me, to reach out and touch my shoulder and command me to stop my washing, to spare her life, but I cannot.

"No, it cannot be." Her tears well and then fall like rain.

Her horror is beating in her chest, causing us both pain, but it is not in panic of her impending death, but for fear of my fate. Fear *for* me, not *of* me, and if I still had a heart, it would have shattered like glass on stone.

Grandmother will die before she makes it back to the castle to warn me of what awaits.

She will fall when her heart gives out, just as she reaches the stream where we once spent so many days, safe beneath the sun and wrapped in the comfort of each other's company. I will find her come morning. Her body still warm, yet already gone. My screams will break the silence of the castle, the village, and the woods that continue to close in around us. But Emer will not give up. Grandmother taught me there is always hope, and Finn had told me about the water in the well.

I am pulled back but I scarcely have time to regain my bearings in my pool before another linen breaks the surface. The moment my head rises from the water, the linen bobs beside me and I am dragged back under into the world of the living.

THE DEATH
OF
FINN O'TOOLE

10

This is Finn's last morning in the world of breath and blood, before my death and after my future had already found him.

I can feel him. All of him.

Every thought that runs wild through his mind.

Every sensation of every hair that stands on the back of his neck, alerting him that something is not right in these woods. The pounding of his strong heart and the coursing of the young, healthy blood through his veins. He is a man in the prime of his life, like a prized stag with many years left to rut. Nothing about his appearance would signal that he is about to die.

The lord had died three days before, and the forest had been buzzing ever since.

Finn thinks it strange that the trees would whisper, and the earth would vibrate under his fingers as he crouches to press his palms into the ground, as he would often do when out to hunt. The dark, moist soil, fertile with the years of decay from fallen leaves, branches, and animals, greedily shifts from the pressure of his fingers to fill the space underneath his nails and between his strong fingers. Almost as if it wants to swallow him up. He is not one for nerves, but something feels off. He knows these woods. He knows its earth. He knows the safest paths and the hidden dangers that lurk should he be careless. Finn is never reckless. Not in the woods, anyway. When he is with Emer, it is a different story.

He has loved Emer since they were children. He is drawn to her like bees are to honey and flies are to rot, unable to be distracted by anything else. And certainly not by the other girls suggested to be a better match. Emer is, after all, only the orphan of a washerwoman. He is reminded often that he is the son of a hunter. Descended from one of the warriors that Cillian had brought with him when they first landed on the island. One of the few cunning enough to survive the first few years as they learned the woods and its hidden dangers. One of the warriors to lay the foundation of the great stone castle that was Cillian's legacy. A castle not built on hard work or conquest, but one built on destiny and a bargain.

Finn's father had spoken to him often of his ancestor Niall, a man of reserve and cleverness. He sat back and observed, whereas many a man would rush in without thought. He saw the look on Cillian's face when he had returned from the woods, claiming to have found the place at which they would build his kingdom. Whereas the others whooped and celebrated, rushing in to clap the back of Cillian, Niall noticed the glassiness of his eyes, the pallor of his skin.

"What happened in there?" he whispered.

"Destiny," responded Cillian.

Niall quietly nodded and remained silent. In the following days and weeks, he set about to learn what had happened to Cillian in those woods. A silent distrust of Cillian and the island grew in him. Something he would pass down through his line, a quiet word and gentle reminder to the sons and daughters who followed.

They would say that Finn was a fine example of the sons that sprang from Niall and his sons. But the truth is that Finn's mother came from the sea. The poor girl had been led no doubt astray by the promise of a sun beam filtered through trees, a song whispered enticingly on the wind, or the smell of something undistinguishable but no less desirable. Finn's father had found her not far from the old well that had supplied them with water when they first laid out the bones of the castle.

She looked as though she had been ravaged, though she would not say by who or what. When he first caught her eye, the woman had a fierceness, a defiance that would challenge any man or spirit. Laying down his bow and spear, he showed her he was of no harm to her and offered her his hand. They stared at each other for some time, neither moving until he finally spoke. "You're safe now, girl. Take my hand, and I will bring you back to the village."

"None of us is safe here," the woman replied. She then laid down her rock and took his hand, allowing him to lead her back to the village.

"Are you from the sea or the castle?" he asked, speaking of the village built as a small port to supply the castle with fish, where ships came and went between this island and the one they had left behind.

"The sea," she said. He had thought as much, for he did not recognize her. She smelled of salt and wind and was unlike any woman he had met before.

It was there in that moment that Finn's father fell in love with Finn's mother. He began to court her, spending more time by the sea than in the forest, earning the ire of the current lord of the castle, Cillian's heir, a dull and indulgent man, obsessed with enlarging the castle beyond what his father had left to him. They never lived long, the sons and heirs of Cillian, often passing once their own sons bloomed into young men.

Finn remains kneeling on the forest floor when a snap of a twig behind him sends an alarm through his senses, telling him danger is near and to run. But Finn knows that to run is to be prey, and that predators enjoy the chase, so he remains fixed where he is, fingers still pressing into the earth.

That is when it begins, the voice from deeper in the wood.

A voice that he knows.

It is singing, and the sorrow that is carried in its notes breaks his heart and commands the tears to fall.

He rises from the ground and begins to follow the song.

One might fancy this a trick, another trap set by the other-folk, but the recognition reaches far beyond Finn's ears. The very tone of the notes burrows deep inside him, until his soul itself begins to vibrate in response.

He had learned long ago, when they tried to use her likeness to lure him into a trap, to find the false notes in her voice and the distortion in her image.

Either his mind has weakened, they have improved their guise, or it is really her. Emer. His love.

He cares not at the moment; he needs only to find her and fix whatever has caused her such sorrow.

The sky begins to darken, and the tree canopy grows thicker.

A mist begins to rise from the cool forest floor, and that is when he sees me.

He doesn't scream or clutch his chest as so many others have before him.

He stares, and I know what he feels; I can taste it. I can see in his eyes the vision that lays before him, just as I had seen in the others.

What the others saw was a frightening hag of loose skin and wrinkles, old, torn clothes, stringy hair, more corpse-like than human.

But Finn sees *me*. He sees through the version of me from the future, from what I had become and turned into from all the washing I had been doing since my death, which, at this moment, from my past and Finn's future, has not occurred yet. He sees all the way to my core, his beloved Emer, the woman he grew up with and fell in love with, in all my beauty and youth.

He knows in his heart that she is in trouble and that he has to save her before it is too late.

I am a warning of his death. He knows the stories.

But he takes it as a warning from me, a fate that he can still prevent.

I know his thoughts; they play in my mind as if they are my own.

If we die, it will be together, and he will do whatever it takes to finish my laundry and end my life as a Bean-nighe. As a washerwoman.

I want to scream. To tell him how he is going to die, that if he runs to the sea, he can be spared, he can live. The castle was already lost because the last heir of Cillian had passed without a child to carry on the bargain. The line had been broken three days before, when Finn had come across Sadhbh.

She was beautiful, unchanged by time as one of the Aos- Síth, the fair folk of the mounds. She was more than just that, she was a Leannan- Síth, one who lives off the life of those who she serves as muse, and she had been feasting off the line of Cillian for centuries.

"Come, cousin," she purred, sensing the selkie blood that ran through Finn's veins, reaching her hand out to him from within the stone circle.

"What is the meaning of this, cousin?" Finn asked cautiously. He knew better than to engage with one such as her, but he could not help himself.

"You are the last of the line of Cillian. Take my hand and let us trade power for power. Let me into your mind, and I will fill your thoughts with potency beyond what you have imagined for yourself."

Her smile was intoxicating, but Finn was immune to her charms and her tricks.

"No." He turned to leave Sadhbh.

"Wait, cousin." Her voice was first urgent, before melting back into smoothness. "It's been so long, let me tell you a story while I wait to be sated. Do you know why the village of salt and sea broke from the castle of wood and springs?"

Finn stopped, cautious but curious.

"The line of Cillian has weakened with each new lord. Their strength of mind and body lessened with each new son. Poor judgments and rash tempers created fissures in a once-strong cornerstone of the kingdom. The village of salt and sea started as a few fishing huts to help feed the castle, and it grew into a village of its own. A village that Cillian's heirs demanded tribute from. The newest lord felt that fish was not enough, and soon a woman was requested as part of his boon. Not just any woman, but a selkie, a creature of the sea. A prize for the lord who had her coat turned into a pair of boots. A prize to show his reach extended beyond that of the land of the island and all the way into the sea itself. The selkie woman was cunning, and on a night when the lord had drunk himself to sleep, she stole the boots and ran into the woods, hoping to make her way back to the sea." She paused for a moment, trying to gauge Finn's reaction, and then continued.

"That is where your father found her, lost in the woods, not far from the well. That is where your father offered her a safe passage, or a safe home. The selkie woman accepted his help, but the lord had already left his mark in her, and when it came time for his child to be born, the selkie mother perished in labor, leaving you, Finn, to the man who had helped her."

"I don't believe you," Finn said. For who could believe such a story?

"You don't need to, cousin, but you know it in your bones. You hear what others don't, you see what they can't." Sadhbh paused long enough for the weight of her words to settle like stone before she whispered, "You are the last heir of Cillian, and his bargain falls to you to carry."

Power asked to be taken, but Finn rejected the beauty and charm of an outstretched hand once more. He left the invitation unmet by the old well.

He turned to leave again, refusing to fall for her charm, walking away as she called out, "The bargain is broken."

Finn didn't turn, didn't acknowledge. He continued to walk because Finn was what Cillian was not: a good man. An honest man. A man who did not strike deals or presume to own what did not belong to him.

Denying her meant that Sadhbh would send her folk to reclaim what was hers. A bargain struck, a bargain broken. The line of Cillian would end with Finn's death and with it, the destruction of the castle.

I know that the ending of our story started long before Finn had rejected her hand, and back to when another man had so foolishly taken it.

THE BINDING
OF
SADHBH AND CILLIAN

11

T he castle had been promised before.

Not just a promise, but a bargain—a deal. One made between man and the other-folk.

I had seen it all as the Bean-nighe that had foretold what awaited Cillian when he had snuck up on me, washing the grave clothes of his lord. I spoke of the island, of a castle, and a kingdom that would last 300 years. I also warned of its fall, of deals struck between man and fae, of what happens when you listen only to beautiful words but not their meaning. But the man cared not what happened in a time when he did not exist. He ignored my warning and set about finding the island.

When Cillian found the island, hidden by mist and waves, he sought to claim it as his own. His first step upon the sandy beach filled him with confidence because he had found his fate. It mattered not to him that the other-folk already inhabited the island. He was protected by destiny and the legacy of the great men who came before him, brave warriors, each with a bold destiny and conquest of their own. He made his way from the beach to the tree line of the lush and green woods of the island. He bade his men to stay behind in the boat and wait for his return at dawn.

Cillian walked proudly into the heavy tree line. It felt to him as though the trees parted, and a pathway revealed itself. *Destiny*, he thought, as each step took him deeper into the woods.

The eerie sounds bothered him not; he knew he was already master here.

The path continued, winding through woods, streams, and piles of rocks that he might have recognized as the ruins of old forts and houses had he paid them any attention.

He walked with confidence, knowing he had already won his prize.

Further and further he walked until he came upon a beautiful woman sitting by a ring of moss-covered rocks.

The woman did not turn to face him. She remained seated within the ring as sunlight filtered down through the leaves, giving her an aura of light. "What is it you've come for?"

"I've come to claim my destiny." Cillian stood tall and arrogant.

"I am Sadhbh, one of the Aos Síth. Tell me of the destiny you seek." Sadhbh stood up and turned to Cillian. She was the most beautiful creature he had ever seen. Just gazing at her filled him with visions of greatness.

"I am here to build a kingdom of my own." He knew it to be true in his bones.

"Take me as your lover, and I will be the lover of the men in your line, and it will be so." Her voice reached out and encircled him, heavy and sweet like honey.

"I already have a wife." Nevertheless, desire coursed through Cillian's veins.

"Not a wife." The fairy woman laughed, moving closer to him, but staying within the bounds of the fairy mound. "For a wife I shall never be again. From this mound you will dig the well that will quench your thirst, and from its waters your visions will spring forth, a kingdom worthy of a lord such as yourself."

"Only a lover?" Cillian briefly wondered what was in it for this woman whose beauty was beyond match, but he didn't dwell on it.

"As a lover only, and as the lover of the men from your line. I will inspire you to build all that you seek, but should the line be broken and the well poisoned with that which you love, then all will fall to ruin and be reclaimed by my kind."

Sadhbh offered her hand to Cillian. A smile spread across her face as he reached inside the rocky circle and took her palm in his. Gently, he led her out from the mound, and there she began to caress his face at once.

She nuzzled her nose and lips into his neck and then stretched her lips up to his ear and whispered, "Tell me of your kingdom."

Cillian shuddered in pleasure, his legs weakening as he slowly sank into the mossy floor of the forest. Sadhbh continued to caress his body, removing his clothing, and urging him to speak the ideas he soon found flooding his mind along with the increasing pleasure the woman brought forth from him. He didn't notice, not yet, that an exchange was happening. That something was carefully being drained from him.

"This is where I'll build my well, and from its waters a great kingdom shall spring," he murmured, taking the woman in and filling her with all of the life he had in him.

"Break the line, poison the well," she whispered in a voice too sweet to be taken as the warning it was meant to be. Her skin glowed more radiant, and the light from that filter through the leaves of the trees created a halo around the woman's figure.

As the woman arched her back and his fingers dug into her hips as she rocked back and forth on top of him, his mind began to care about what happened after him. Suddenly, his bloodline and ensuring it didn't break mattered. It was the only thing that mattered.

And the dark woods, which had waited patiently for another bargain to be struck, began to stir, too quiet for anyone to notice.

THE DEATH
OF
EMER O'TOOLE

12

T he wood did not fall gently to sleep after the bargain was broken.

What began as gentle stirrings of something ancient beneath its roots and stones were now a raging current. What had been waiting centuries with patience for this moment emerged fully from the shadows. The air thickened and the paths shifted.

This is where my story ends, when I stopped being Emer, and my journey as the washerwoman truly begins.

The forest erupted in the chittering of creatures who had awakened long ago, whose darkness blossomed into something ugly, no longer hidden. Disappearances had begun earlier in the year, and fear had taken root once the lord's health declined more noticeably and his obsession with his bloodline and making an heir grew. He had failed to produce a known living heir, and everyone believed Cillian's line would end with him.

The darkness that grew, the disappearances, none of it was enough to keep me from trying to save my grandmother. I could not accept that she was gone. I remembered what Finn had said about the well and the stories about the magic of its waters. If there was even a chance I could see her again, I would try, and no one would stop me.

I run until I reach the place where the well lies, just beyond a ring of moss-covered stones encircling the ruined remains of its old stone base. I stop only to catch my breath, the ceramic jug under one arm, when a strong hand grabs me.

"What are you doing here?" Finn looks at me in alarm.

"The well. Grandmother said its water had magic and healing properties, I just—"

"Don't EVER do that again!" Finn screams. He lets go of his tight grip on my arm, causing me to fall onto the hard ground. I lie there, in surprise. Finn has never raised his hand or his voice at me, ever. The sting of his grip on my arm is a shock to my body.

"You're not my lord nor my master!" I hiss back. I push myself up off the ground, approach him and strike him across the cheek. No one will stop me from taking the water and using it to see my grandmother again. I will fight until my last breath to see her.

I move to hit him again, but he catches my hand. "Don't ever do that again."

He takes me by the wrist and drags me back to the village and out of the woods. "You don't understand how close you just were to death."

It turns out he was right, and that was the last time I saw Finn.

We made it back to the village, and I returned to my grandmother's house. It still smelled like her, and I sat on the floor, rocking myself back and forth and looking at the door. Waiting for her to walk through it again, though I knew she never would. Since the morning I found her body, it felt like the darkness from the woods was closing in on us. Fear began to grow from the coldness that had seeped into my bones from her absence. Every time Finn went to the woods to hunt, panic gripped me that he would be the next one swallowed up by the woods. If I could see her, summon her spirit from the waters in the well, then maybe I could feel safe again. But now, now I was totally alone. Finn went back to his father's place. It felt like the end for us, like the end of everything for me.

And it would be the end, but not because our love was broken, but because I never listened.

In the early morning hours the next day, I snuck back out into the woods.

I found my way back on the path to the well.

Instead of magic and healing waters, I found the destiny that I was cursed to. I knew if I had turned back as Finn demanded, I would be safe at home and in no danger, but guilt has always beaten louder than fear. I just needed to see Grandmother again. To tell her I was sorry for not finding her in time to save her. To hear her voice tell me that everything was going to be okay, to not be afraid.

I was so occupied with drawing the water that I didn't hear her, the fairy woman.

I don't know that it would have changed my fate even if I did.

Her lips whisper in my ear, "Poison the well with that which you loved. Tell me, Emer, what chore did you not finish? What linen did you let escape your grasp, unwashed and for no one to find?"

As the pressure builds on my neck, the faint chants begin.

"Death only opens the door, sweet Emer, remember that what you've left undone is what has locked you inside," Sadhbh whispers amongst the growing voices of the dark ones she has called up.

"Steal the rocks and burn the stone.
Split the skulls and crush the bones.
Destroy the village and poison the well.
Muffle the shrieks and leave no one to tell."

I hear Finn scream as my neck snaps and my body falls backward, then down into the well.

The Bargain Broken

13

Before his death, Finn saw it all. And as the Bean-nighe who washed his grave clothes, I saw all that he did.

He was up earlier than usual, unable to sleep and restless with worry.

His heart dropped when he came by my grandmother's house and found it empty.

He knew where I would be—that I would seek the well once more on the promise of an old wives' tale that said I could conjure a departed loved one for one final goodbye and finish what was left unsaid.

The threat of Sadhbh still rang within his head and heart.

He ran into the woods, toward the well, praying that he would find me before anything happened. His distrust of the woods had only grown in these passing moons.

That's when he saw Sadhbh with her arms around my neck.

How easily and with little effort it took to break my neck and send me down the well.

"It's a shame," Sadhbh called out to him. "You would have made for such good feeding, your power and possibility. Such a waste." She sighed as her voice faded and the other voices grew louder.

He heard them, the same ones he had heard in the woods since the last lord's health started to fail. He knew what was coming, Sadhbh had told him. The bargain was broken because of him, the last heir of Cillian who was still alive, but who refused to inherit the curse and feed the Leannan Síth .

Blood didn't matter to Sadhbh the way it mattered in the castle, only whether the bargain could still find a carrier. Sadhbh had always known that eventually the bargain would be broken; she had counted on the fact that it would. She did not count on the fact that it would be willfully broken by that of a good-hearted man, though. And while she had won the bargain, she had lost because Finn had rejected her. She called forth her folk, the dark malevolent beings of the woods, to reclaim what she had lent out. They came in force, dark shadows racing through the trees toward the village.

Finn knew what my fate was; he had already seen me as the Bean-nighe.

He knew what he had to do.

He ran, ran to the bank of the stream where I washed clothes and to the spot I had lost the last piece of Liera's linen. The laundry that had become my own when my grandmother had transferred the task to me.

I had damned myself.

Finn would die, though.

He was destined to die just as I was destined to become the Bean-nighe.

He reached the stream just as the shrieks began to rise from the village and smoke thickened within the castle walls. He called for his hawk, for his ancestors and the helpers who dwelled within the woods.

Together, he and the hawk set to the task of finding the linen lost all those years ago. Finn prayed to all that was good that they would find it, and he knew in his bones that they would not be forsaken. For all the evil that lived in the woods and the wider world, he knew good endured as well. He trusted his ancestors to guide him and keep him safe, and as he did, the wind shifted. His hawk screeched when he found what they had been looking for.

As Finn ran after the hawk for the old linen, a redcap struck, cutting into his stomach with a stab and a twist before leaving him for dead.

Finn stood where the small man had wounded him, fighting to stay upright before his strength gave out and he dropped to his knees. He lifted his gaze to the sky, the hawk screeching above him as if urging him not to give up. Finn pitched forward. He clawed into the earth as his legs dragged weakly behind him, and he crawled to the spot, blood streaking the ground in his wake.

As his strength drained, he managed to call for the hawk. It flew to him with what looked to be nothing more than an old, dirty rag in its beak, dropping it at his feet.

Finn grasped it and dragged himself the short distance to the water. With what little strength he had left, he began to wash.

He wrung the linen out, fighting the pull of death's embrace.

When he was finished, he hauled himself upright, staggered to the line, and hung the linen before collapsing to the ground. He did not claim it—the work left undone. He only finished it.

"Finn." My voice comes first as a sorrowful echo, calling from the stream.

"Finn, my love." The words ring out from the voice that was once lost and is now my own again. A lightness overtakes me as the weight of the curse, of all I have carried, slips free and sinks into the stream, settling into the mud.

I am no longer a monster, but as I was when I died. Young, beautiful, and loved as I had been all along, even when I had forgotten it. The well didn't punish wickedness, only what was unfinished. And Finn finished the final linen, he made the unfinished whole. The well had nothing left to bind me.

He lifts a blood-streaked hand toward me, a weak smile on his lips, an acceptance that the price of his life was worth every moment. As though he would happily die a thousand times over to buy my freedom.

"Thank you." I reach out and take his hand, lifting his spirit from his body to join mine as we are encompassed by a light so bright that no darkness could ever come close to touching it.

We walk back towards the woods, leaving his body behind. The trees are no longer dark, but bright and evergreen. Not a trap, but a promise.

Each step feels like forgiveness and our world set right. In the end, it was Finn whose heart could not be bought or swayed. In the end, it was my ability to accept his love and forgive myself for my mistakes and selfishness that played a part in both our deaths.

In the end, we agreed that fate, bargains, and ancestors be damned.

The screams from the village fade into the background as we walk into a new eternity of light and love together. The afterlife I have desired is finally mine.

Glossary

Below you will find a list of terms and how they are used in this story which may differ from the original meaning in order to fit the story.

Selkie - A mythological being that takes the form of a seal. However, it can transform into a human by shedding its "coat" or seal skin.

Bean-nighe - A cursed fairy spirit of women who died either in childbirth or with unfinished laundry, seen at streams washing the blood stained clothes of those destined to die.

Aos-sìth - A beautiful race of fairy folk, similar to elves.

Leannan- sìth- A beautiful malevolent fairy woman of the Aos-sìth. She takes human lovers and becomes their muse.

Baobhan-sìth- A malevolent fairy, similar to a vampire, who appears as a beautiful woman in a green dress.

Red caps - A malevolent murderous goblin who wears a cap stained red from the blood of those they kill.

JKDIVIA